JERI TELSTAR

AND THE GIRL WHO WALKED BACKWARDS

Chapter one

DRRRRRNG! THE BELL RANG. It was lunch break. The classroom doors burst open and objects moving at the speed of light shot out into the corridors and raced for the staircases.

In less than a minute, all the speeding missiles, laughing and chattering, had reached the playground.

All except two boys in the last classroom on the third floor. They emerged in slow motion, travelling at the speed of glaciers that had stayed up too late watching movies.

That's because they were rather nervous about what was going to happen in the playground. You see, a kid called Morris Maurice had started a secret club called The Secret Club. You could only join if you revealed something to the other members. Not just any old thing: you had to share something hidden that was mega important.

Two boys, Jeremiah Lee and Prakash Das, had been invited to join. They were due to be interviewed that lunch break. The pair had been told to meet the group at the south corner of the playground. Both of them were really nervous. They slowly descended the staircase, eyes cast down at their feet.

Above them, the sky was grey, dark and full of clouds. It matched their mood as they ambled at a snail's pace to the corner of the playground.

"Are you ready for this?" Prakash asked.

Jeremiah shook his head. "No. I don't like the idea of sharing secrets with a big group of people. I mean, the whole point of a secret is that only one or maybe two people know it."

Prakash said, "Yeah. That's true. But joining a secret club is kind of cool. So I guess it might be worth it."

"Maybe," said Jeremiah. "Let's see."

They walked past the infants' playhouse and saw a group of about 20 youngsters of various ages standing in the corner.

Morris Maurice, a tall, thin young man in ill-fitting clothes, greeted them. "Welcome, potential newbies," he said. "Come and stand among us."

The two boys walked nervously into the circle.

"Now you know the rules," Morris said. "You can only be a member of the club if you tell us a secret, something which—"

"It's gotta be a good one," interrupted a girl called Loretta Ting. "Somefing really juicy and shocking."

Both newcomers gulped.

Morris took a big, padlocked book out of a bag. "This is The Secret Club's *Book of Secrets*. Your secrets will be added and you will be able to read other members' secrets if you are accepted. Do you understand?"

Jeremiah and Prakash nodded.

"Okay, let's get on with it," said Loretta. "Who's going first?"

Prakash put up his hand. "Me. I wanna get it

over with."

Silence descended and all eyes were on him. "Well," he said. "I never told anyone this before, but . . ." He paused for effect. "I don't like chocolate cake. Or ice cream."

Morris and Loretta glanced at each other.

"Is that it?" Loretta said.

Prakash nodded.

Morris shook his head. "That's not good enough," he said.

"That's *feeble*," added Loretta.

Prakash's forehead wrinkled. "Okay, let me think of something else."

"It better be good," Morris said.

"Um," Prakash bit his lip. "Er. How about this: I cheated in a spelling test once. I had the hard ones written on my hand."

"Useless," said Loretta. "You're out, Prakash. Next." She turned her gaze to Jeremiah.

"No, wait." Prakash lifted his hands. "Give me one more chance. I've got one."

Morris folded his arms and looked cross. "This is your last chance. You have ten seconds. Nine. Eight."

Prakash blurted out: "I really, really like a girl called, er, Sophie, in the classroom opposite. I wrote a poem for her once, and slipped it into her bag."

Loretta's eyebrows shot up. "A love poem?"

"Kind of," said Prakash.

"Did she reply?" Loretta asked.

"Um, yes," said Prakash.

Morris asked, "What was the reply?"

"She said, 'I love you too, darling Prakash.'"

Morris nodded. Loretta smiled.

"Okay," they said at the same time. "Not bad. You're in."

Loretta, screwing up her mouth to help her concentrate, carefully wrote the secret into the book. Prakash, giving a sigh of relief, joined the circle. Several people patted him on the back as he found a spot with the other members.

Jeremiah's eyes had widened at the

conversation that had just passed. He knew that there was no girl called Sophie in the classroom opposite, and Prakash had an over-active imagination.

"Now your turn, Jeremiah Lee," said Morris. "Can you give us a better secret than Prakash?"

"I don't think so," he said.

"Well, try," said Loretta.

"You must know something shocking," added Morris.

"Okay," said Jeremiah. "How about this: I really, really, *really* like . . . mathematics. I've read every maths book in the school. I get extra maths homework from Mr Gee because I ask for it."

There was a gasp from the onlookers. Kids clamped hands over their mouths in shock. Loretta's eyes widened. Morris said, "You can't be serious."

Jeremiah nodded. "It's true," he said. "In fact, I would go so far as to say that I *love* maths lessons. I live for them. But I also like science, probably just as much." He warmed to his theme. "Actually, you know, I love homework of any kind. I can't get enough of it."

Two children fainted.

"Eww!" said Loretta. "That's disgusting. That's sick. You're the weirdest person I've ever met."

"He's a swot," said a child in the circle.

"He's a geek," said another.

"He's a nerd," said a third.

The circle widened as everyone stepped back, as if Jeremiah was carrying some sort of disease.

Morris shook his head. "Sorry, mate," he said. "That's really very sick indeed. No way are you joining this club. I mean—"

"That's all right," said Jeremiah. "I really don't mind."

At that moment, a police car sped past the school, its lights flashing and its siren wailing. Then fireworks burst in the sky.

Jeremiah said, "Look, I gotta go. See you later," and he turned and ran.

***

Forty seconds later, Jeremiah was hidden in a space behind the bicycle shed. He took out a face mask and a communicator device from a secret pocket in his backpack. Slipping the mask over his eyes, he dialled a number.

The face of Frank, the local fire chief, appeared on screen. "Ah, Jeri," he said. "Thanks for getting back to me. There's a crisis at the electricity power plant. We need your help urgently."

"How can I help?"

"We have a *big* problem. There's a dripping tap at the electricity plant."

On the communicator's tiny screen, Frank moved aside to show that he was standing outside the electricity plant for the district of Utter Backwater. It was a large, stately-looking block with no windows, and lots of wires and tubes snaking out in all directions.

"A dripping tap? That doesn't seem like a big problem," Jeremiah said.

The fireman's face filled the screen again. "Let me give you the full story. Some villain sneaked into the top floor of the power plant. There's practically nothing up there except the water storage tank. He ripped the cover off the tank. The water tank is full, right up to the brim. A leaky tap is about to drip into it, and we can't shut it off. You can see why we're worried."

Jeremiah pictured the scene. If the tap dripped into the tank, it would overflow. Liquid would spill down into the machinery, and the whole electricity plant would short circuit. At best, there would be no electricity for the whole district until it was fixed and dried out. At worst, there could be an explosion that would destroy the power plant for ever.

"Can't you turn off the main water pipe that takes water into the building?"

Frank nodded. "We can. But that's the problem. It's buried. The villain covered it with cement. We're digging down to it, and it will take at least an hour."

"Do you have that long?"

"No," said the fire chief. "That tank is full to the

brim. If one drop of water gets added to it, it will overflow. Water will hit the electricity generation equipment below it, and boom!"

"I'll be there as soon as I can," said Jeremiah. "Over and out."

Jeremiah whipped his mask off, and tapped the memory button to call his grandmother. It took five seconds for the screen to light up with the face of an elderly woman. She looked cross.

"Nan, I need to—"

She interrupted: "Jeremiah, you know you are not allowed to phone me from school. I don't care what you have to say. It can wait until school's over."

"But Grandma Nan, there's a big problem at the power plant. The fire chief wants me to go and help immediately."

She shook her head. "You know the rules," she said. "School comes first. Saving the world comes second. We need to keep our priorities straight. Over and out."

The screen went black.

Jeremiah sighed. His grandmother was *so* strict. Other superheroes didn't have these problems. Why should he?

He opened up the secret pocket in his backpack again and looked at his superhero gear. He saw his nano-engine boots, which could propel him into the air. He saw his mask, with its built-in vision magnifier. He saw his costume, which had a framework of tiny motors built into it to give him super-strength.

He pressed the "on" button on the costume's belt and everything glowed purple as it powered up.

Then his wrist communicator came to life again. Grandma Nan appeared, saying, "And if you are thinking of disobeying me, I just want to tell you that I am remotely cutting all power to your super-suit until school's over."

The purple glow and rising hum of the suit powering up was instantly replaced by the yellow glow and falling note of the suit powering down.

Jeremiah Lee was powerless.

Just then, he felt a splotch of water on his face. While he had been on the phone, the sky had darkened. It was beginning to rain. It reminded him of the single drip that could blow up the entire power plant. He had to do something. But what?

Chapter two

JEREMIAH LEE SNEAKED OUT of the school gate and ran down the road. He knew he would get into *huge* trouble if anyone saw him, so he raced from tree to tree, keeping his head low.

Once out of sight of the school, he ran breathlessly along the pavements. Oh, if only Grandma Nan wasn't so hard on him! With his superhero boots on, he could have made the journey in seconds. But on foot it would take several minutes – time he could not afford to waste, given the danger that the power plant was in.

Still, he knew he mustn't complain. Grandma Nan ran a secret group called Nan-O-Technology with a team of other old women, and they had made him a costume using nanotechnology, the science of tiny machines, to give him special powers.

But she was very strict. He was banned from doing any superhero-type work during school hours. Even in the evenings and weekends he was often prevented from saving the world until he had finished his homework.

At last he reached the gates of the power station. He stopped behind a tree and quickly put on his costume. Although it had been remotely powered down, it still looked mostly the same. As long as no one asked him to fly, or show off his super-strength, he would at least look right.

Seconds later, he was no longer Jeremiah Lee, small, puny schoolboy.

Now he was Jeri Telstar, small, puny superhero.

There was a police cordon at the gates to the plant. Jeremiah ran towards the door.

"Woah, young man," said the officer at the gate. "Where do you think you're going? No one allowed inside."

"I'm a superhero," Jeri said, gesturing towards his costume and cape.

"Maybe so, but you're not allowed in. It's very dangerous."

"I *know* it's very dangerous. That's why I'm here. I'm a superhero. *Think*."

The officer thought for a moment. He took half a step backwards, half inclined to let the boy in.

Not wanting to waste a second, Jeri raced past him. "I have to go in. I'm here to save everyone."

"Wait," said the officer.

"Look, I'll make sure you won't get into trouble for this," Jeri called back over his shoulder.

"Oh, okay, thanks," said the policeman, relaxing.

Inside, Jeri found himself in a massive room, full of large tanks and machines and tubes and pipes and monitors.

But the few people inside were all staring upwards. Jeri followed their line of sight and realised that they were all staring at the top level of a network of internal staircases.

Just under the roof of the building was a big water tank. Standing on a platform nearby were several people, including fire chief Frank and a woman in a white coat, who looked like some sort of scientist.

"Hey, it's Jeri Telstar," he heard someone say next to him.

He turned to bow to his fans.

"Are you going to fly up there and save the situation?" one of the ground level staff asked.

"I think I'll take the stairs," said Jeri. "To save energy."

"Good idea," said the man. "After all, if this plant gets destroyed, there's going to be a big shortage of energy."

Jeri ran up the metal staircase. The building was four storeys tall, so it was a long climb to the water tank and he was puffed out when he got there.

Frank smiled to see him. "Glad you could make it so fast, Jeri. It's a tricky situation. The water tank is full to the top and we're worried that it will overflow. The tank is so full that if we disturb the water even slightly, a few drops are likely to spill over the edge – and the tiniest splash could be enough to short circuit that thing below us."

He pointed to the huge machine beneath them, which was fizzing and crackling. "That's the heart of the system: the tank where they store the electricity before pumping it down the cables into the sockets in people's homes. If a drop of water hits that . . . "

Frank did not need to finish the sentence. Jeri could imagine what would happen: a massive short circuit, an explosion and the blacking out of the whole city.

"Now look up," said Frank. "That's what we're really worried about."

Above the water tank, a network of pipes stretched across the ceiling. And at the junction of two pipes, Jeri could see dampness glinting at the nozzle of a tap.

"That looks bad," the boy said.

The fireman nodded. "It's a tiny leak, but it's only a matter of time before it turns into a drip of water. And then we're done for."

Suddenly, they could hear a commotion below them.

At ground level, the doors burst open. Four people in formal clothes entered. The two men wore black tuxedos and the two women wore long, dark dresses. All four carried musical instruments.

The police guard who had been at the door followed, looking rather nervous. Jeri wondered why he had let them through.

The four musicians set up folding seats and music stands and started to play.

"What's going on?" said the fire chief.

"I couldn't stop them," shouted the officer who had been guarding the door. "They were very insistent."

Jeri said: "It sounds like they're playing TV theme music."

Next to Frank was a scientist named Professor Yvonne Brain. She said: "Don't you watch TV?

That's the theme song for *Musclehead*, the superhero show."

"Oh no," said Frank. "You know what that means?"

"What?" Jeri asked.

"It means Musclehead himself is on the way. He always sends his people ahead of him so that they can play his signature tune when he arrives."

At that moment, there was a huge crashing sound. Daylight suddenly appeared through the wall on the left and a large, muscular man flew into the building, biceps bulging.

"Fear not," he bellowed. "Musclehead is here."

The bodybuilder-turned-superhero landed heavily on the platform where the others were standing, causing it to creak and tremble.

"Where there's trouble, there's Musclehead," he said. "Now, ladies and gentlemen, stand back and allow me to solve the problems of the world, as I usually do."

"Be careful," said Professor Brain. "It's really

important that no water splashes out of the tank onto the equipment below. Otherwise everything will blow up. And it is already brimming over."

"Easy," said the large superhero. "All I need to do is put my huge, muscular arms into the tank and slosh out some of the water."

"No," she said. "Not one drop must fall to the ground."

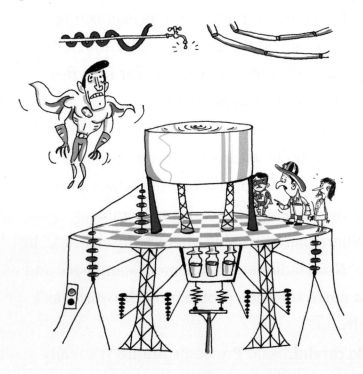

"Not a problem," said Musclehead. "I'll find some sort of giant bucket and scoop the water out. Hmm. Let me see."

He leaped off the platform and flew around the power plant. Finding a large vat-shaped object on the second level, he wrenched it out of the ground and flew back to the platform.

"This will do," he said, landing heavily on the platform again. "With this huge metal bucket I will scoop the water out. Problem solved."

Frank started to say the word "wait" – but someone with a much louder voice said it first: "*Wait!*"

Musclehead turned round. "What's up?" he said.

Below them, at ground level, a breathless small woman in dark glasses carrying a megaphone appeared downstairs. Behind her was a camera crew. "Can you turn to the left when you dip the giant bucket into the water tank, so that we can get a better view?"

"It's the news crew," Musclehead explained to the fireman and the scientist. "Pretty much everything I do is newsworthy, so these guys follow me around." He changed angle. "Is that better, sweetheart?"

"Better," she said. "Okay. Rolling. Action."

Musclehead picked up his huge bucket and flew up to the edge of the water tank.

"No, wait," said Professor Brain. "It's too risky. When you put the edge of the bucket in, you'll displace some of the water and it will splash over the side."

"What?" said Musclehead.

"Stop. We have to find another way."

"But this way will look really good," Musclehead objected. "Me holding huge metal things always looks good."

"But you'll destroy the whole plant, and maybe the whole town," the scientist complained.

Reluctantly, Musclehead stopped. He came back to the platform and lowered the bucket.

"Look lady, I'll give you one minute to think of a better solution. Otherwise we do it my way," he said.

Standing quietly watching this scene was Jeri.

His eyes darted from side to side as his brain worked. The concept of "displacing" water reminded him of something he had read in a homework book. "Tell me more about displacing water," he asked the scientist.

"Later," Professor Brain said. "We're all kind of busy now."

Jeri took out his backpack, which he kept tucked behind his cloak, then found his science homework. Looking up displacement in the index at the back, he flipped through the pages to find the story of Archimedes.

The text said: "Archimedes was asked to find a way to work out the mass of the king's crown. As he lowered himself into his bath, his body displaced a certain amount of water. The line of water around the bath moved upwards. Then he worked out that any item dropped into water displaced it to an extent that exactly matched its volume."

"Look, guys. If you can't think of anything else to do, I'll try with my mega bucket," Musclehead said, lifting it up again as the cameras rolled beneath them.

Jeri said: "No. As soon as you put the bucket into the water, the level will rise and some of the water will slop over the edge. It's the Archimedes principle."

There was some chuckling below. The news team found it amusing to see the enormous superhero being told how to do his job by the small child with a cape and mask.

"Hey, kid, no one seems to have a better idea," said Musclehead.

"Wait," said Jeri. "I've got one."

Jeri scampered up the ladder and peered into the tank.

"So, do you think staring into the tank will

solve the problem?" Musclehead asked.

"No," said Jeri. "I'm just investigating a theory I've formed after looking at my school science book."

Frank's eyebrows rose. "I appreciate that homework is important, Jeri, but I think you ought to concentrate on fixing the problem before you—"

"Interesting," the boy said. "This is not tap water. It's a tank of salt water. I can see lots of salt crystals at the bottom of it. It must have been set up for flushing the toilets, before it got blocked and forgotten. Also, there seems to be some sort of built-in stirring device in the tank."

"So what?" said Musclehead. "How's that going to help?"

Just then there was a shout from the scientist. "It's too late," Professor Brain said. "Look."

They all looked up.

A large drop of water had formed on the dripping tap – and was about to fall into the water tank.

"We'd better run!" she said.

Musclehead grinned. "Now, let me do it my way," he said.

"No," said Jeri. "I've got a plan. I'm going to stir the water and see what happens."

"Isn't that a bit risky?" said Frank.

Jeri shouted down: "If I stir it just enough to make the salt crystals dissolve, the water level won't rise."

The scientist nodded. "I think I understand what he's doing. If there's water on top of salt, and the two elements are stirred together, the overall volume won't go up – it could actually go down."

Jeri gently used the built-in stirrer to churn up the water, hoping that he could dissolve the salt without breaking the surface tension.

There was a tense silence for half a minute as Jeri stirred, and saw the salt crystals at the bottom of the tank start to dissolve.

Just then, the drop of water fell from the tap and landed with a tiny *splot* in the middle of the water tank. But the level of water in the tank had already fallen slightly, and it was easily absorbed.

The fire chief shook his head. "Amazing. That's like magic."

"It's not magic," said Jeri. "It's science."

Jeri continued to stir the water in the tank. The water level continued to fall.

Then he took a long, loose thread from his fraying suit and threw it over the leaky pipe. "If more drips come down, they'll run along the thread," Jeri said. "You can catch them in your helmet, Fireman Frank."

The scientist clapped.

Musclehead lowered his bucket.

Chapter three

BACK AT SCHOOL, JEREMIAH raced into the classroom. He sat down, breathless.

His school teacher, Mrs Suklemon, eyed him with undisguised irritation.

"You are 15 minutes late, Lee. Do you have more important things to do than coming to class?" she said. "What were you doing?"

"I was, um, in the toilet," said Jeremiah. This was true – he had raced back to school, run through the empty playground and hidden in the toilet to change.

"You need to get your priorities right, young man," she said. "What society needs is young people who can make a difference. Not children who spend their time idling in the toilets."

"Sorry, miss," said Jeremiah. "I won't be late again."

He took out his books and started looking at the

chapter the class was working on. But he found it hard to concentrate. His mind was filled with the scene at the power plant.

And particularly the expression on the face of Musclehead.

The massive superhero had been furious when it became obvious that his answer to the problem had done nothing but endanger everyone, while Jeri's had saved the day.

"You call that superhero-ing?" he had shouted at Jeri. "You cheated. You used stuff out of a book. You didn't use super-strength or anything."

"There's no rules that you have to solve every problem with super-strength," Jeri said.

"Oh yes there is," Musclehead countered.

"Where?"

"Everyone knows that superheroes solve problems with their fists and their super-strength and their heat-vision and stuff. We hit bad guys and we tear up the town. That's what we do. We don't get stuff out of *homework books*. You're fouling up the system."

"Sorry," said Jeri.

The scientist, Professor Brain, had stepped in front of Musclehead. "Kindly stop shouting at Master Telstar. Not only is he our local superhero, but he saved the day. Your methods would have blown the place up."

Musclehead had turned red with fury. "You don't talk to me like that, lady," he hollered. "I'm a celebrity."

"You broke part of my electricity plant," she complained, pointing to the huge metal cylinder he had broken off to use as a giant bucket.

"Exactly," said Musclehead. "Who else could have done that? No one. Only me. I am 100 per cent muscle."

"Including between your ears," she said.

"That's right," he said. "And I'm not ashamed of it."

She rolled her eyes upwards. "Typical," she said.

The angry superhero had turned to face Jeri. "I'm going to get you for this, Telstar, or whatever your name is. See if I don't. I'm going to report you at the meeting of superheroes next week."

"There's a meeting of superheroes?" asked Jeri.

"Yes. But it's top secret," said Musclehead. "I'm not surprised that you don't know anything about it, since you are no hero at all."

A voice called out from the floor below them. "When and where does it take place?" it said.

"Next Thursday, on the island of—" Musclehead stopped himself. "Hey – it's secret. I just told you. No details."

The news crew, who had filmed the entire dispute, were clearly amused by the scene.

Roaring with anger, Musclehead flew out of the building through the hole in the wall he had created on his arrival.

The scientist tutted. "So unnecessary! Why smash a hole in the wall when there are perfectly good doors downstairs?"

Sitting at his desk, Jeremiah couldn't help but think about the superheroes' meeting.

He had not been a hero for long, and was less than half the age of most other costumed crime fighters, but he was serious about his hobby, and was considering being a full-time hero when he grew up.

He'd love to be invited to a gathering of heroes. It would make him feel like the real thing. And also, he would get to meet some of his own personal heroes.

When the bell rang for the close of the school day, Jeremiah went home still deep in thought.

He entered the cottage through the front door to find Grandma Nan standing there, a stern look on her face.

"Hi, Grandma," he said.

"I've just heard the radio news bulletin," she said. "You went out at lunchtime and rescued the power plant, didn't you?"

Jeremiah bit his lip. He felt guilty. "Yes, but Grandma, I didn't do any superhero-ing," he said. "I just solved it from something I read in my science book. Really. Honest. So it was more like extended school work than hero work."

She continued to gaze at him.

He went on: "I didn't use my superpowers – you know I didn't, because you powered my suit down."

Slowly, Grandma Nan smiled. "I know what happened. I heard all about it from Frank." She rubbed his hair. "I'm proud of you. And just to show how pleased I am, I am going to let you have the power back on for an hour, before you settle down to do your homework."

"Wow, thanks, Grandma," he said. "I wouldn't mind a bit of a fly around. It helps me clear the cobwebs out of my mind and wakes me up after an afternoon stuck in the classroom."

Chapter four

FLYING HIGH IN THE SKY, Jeri Telstar soared over Utter Backwater.

No one could say that it was an important town. It was just the crossroads of a few major streets that ran between the larger cities of the region. To the east was the large city of Sprawl, and to the west was the coastline, which was dominated by the seaside town of Saltwinds.

But, from above, Utter Backwater had its own beauty. The streets and houses formed interesting geometric shapes. The farms and allotments made a chequerboard pattern. The rivers and hills that surrounded the town gave it a feeling of timelessness, as if nothing had changed for centuries.

Using his nano-engined boots to stand high in the sky, Jeri saw the town's borders, where the clusters of buildings gave way to green fields and farmland. He saw the way the canal, which looked so straight when you were walking beside it, actually curved and wound around in loops. He saw horses galloping at top speed around the grounds of the riding stable. He saw people heading home from school and from work – tiny dots on the pavements.

But then his eye was caught by a figure in white, moving along a hillside at the southern edge of town. Why would someone be going hill-walking now, as the day was coming to an end? The figure was on a path that led to a mountain ridge. There were no buildings for several kilometres in either direction. He flew down to get a closer look.

As he approached, he saw that the figure was small, and was walking backwards. He blinked. That couldn't be right. But he looked again. For sure, someone was walking steadily backwards along the path.

He lowered himself further and came to rest at the top of a tall poplar tree at the edge of the field.

He saw a young girl, about his own age.

Puzzled, he used the zoom-function built into his mask to get a closer look.

She was walking at normal speed, but in a backwards direction. She didn't seem to be bothered about bumping into things, and was moving purposefully through the field. It didn't seem to trouble her that she wouldn't be able to see where she was going. She had pale hair, almost white in colour, and wore light-coloured clothes and dark sunglasses.

Eccentric, he thought to himself.

Not wanting to spy on anyone, he clicked his heels together and soared back into the sky.

***

Half an hour later, Jeri was heading home. He had enjoyed his time in the air, and had gone to the edge of Saltwinds, but it was hard to fly straight in gusty winds from the sea, and he was soon getting tired.

Landing in a wood near his home, he let himself into the cottage and went to his room to take off his superhero costume and get into his casual clothes.

Grandma called up to him, "By the way, while you were out, a man delivered a letter for you. It looks like an invitation to something. It's on the hall table."

Jeremiah raced downstairs and snatched up a fat letter. Could this be his invitation to the superhero gathering that Musclehead had mentioned? There had been several articles about him in the paper. Maybe the organisers had read about him and tracked him down!

He was so anxious to get the letter open that he fumbled with the envelope and dropped it a couple of times before he could get it open.

It *was* an invitation. *"You are invited to join the Nerds Round Table, the annual gathering of the most unrepentant swots and geeks in the region,"* it said. *"This is a great honour. We will also be contacting your school."*

Oh no, thought Jeremiah. This will do no good at all for my popularity level.

***

The next day, school started with a surprise.

Halfway through morning assembly, the headmaster, Mr Ning, introduced a new girl. "Please welcome a new member of the school, Ms Miranda Tuck," he said. "Please stand up, Miss Tuck."

The young woman with the pale, whitish hair that Jeremiah had seen walking backwards on the hills the previous day rose to her feet. She was still wearing a large, wide pair of tinted glasses. She didn't smile or nod or acknowledge the polite applause that broke out but simply stood for a few seconds and then sat down again.

Mr Ning read out a few notes about the new

student. "Miranda is a quiet, studious and bookish girl, according to her previous teachers, and will be a credit to the school when it comes to exam time. Her interests are reading and dancing. She enjoys maths and science too. I hope you will give her a warm welcome."

Jeremiah was intrigued. He knew that "quiet, studious and bookish" was likely to be teacher-talk for "nerd". And how come her listed interests did not include "walking backwards by herself on the hills"?

As the assembly wore on, he went back to thinking about his own problems. He was cross with himself for not having realised that confessing his love for books and studying would cause such a bad reaction from the members of The Secret Club. Anyway, he'd better make sure that his invitation to the geek gathering next week was kept well hidden.

At lunch break, he saw Miranda Tuck walk straight to a bench at the side of the playground and sit down, gazing at people through her dark glasses.

He went over to her. "Hi," he said. "I'm Jeremiah. I'm in your year group, but not in your class. I heard your interests include reading and stuff. Me too. Are you new in town?"

"Yeah," she said. "My dad moved here to work."

"Do you like it here?"

"No. I'm used to the big city. This town is so small and quiet. It's like nowhere land."

Jeremiah nodded.

She added, "I've never lived in the countryside before. It smells."

"I used to live in the city," Jeremiah said. "But I moved here a few months ago and I didn't like it at first. But I really enjoy it now. It's funny but you get to know more people in a small town than you do in a big city."

She didn't reply.

He couldn't think of anything else to say. He wondered if he should mention that he had seen her walking backwards on the ridge. But he didn't want to seem strange or creepy, so he said nothing.

"Well, see you around," he said, rising and walking away.

Before lunch break was over, he saw Roland Boot standing in the middle of a crowd of young people. Roland was the school gossip and rumour-monger. He was famous for spreading weird stories about his classmates, almost all of them completely untrue.

As Jeremiah approached, the group went quiet. Roland glanced up at him and then stopped talking.

Jeremiah decided that the smartest thing to do was to keep walking and stroll right past them.

He went over to the sports area to watch people playing a lunch-time game of basketball. Five minutes later, he was approached by one of his best friends, a red-haired girl called Merry Weather. Merry was a hard-working swot too, but

she wasn't as extreme as Jeremiah, and somehow managed to be popular at the same time. She was going on a school trip with the netball team for a week, and he knew he would miss her.

"I see Roland is sharing stories again," he said.

She rolled her eyes.

"Was it something about me?" Jeremiah asked. "I noticed how he went quiet when I walked past."

"Don't worry," said Merry. "It wasn't exactly about you. He was saying that scientists had discovered that geekishness was contagious. He was saying that if you touch the skin of a geek, you become a bit more geekish yourself."

"But that's really stupid."

"Of course it's stupid," she said. "But you know what Roland is like. Anyway, he was just saying that we have to be careful of geeks, when you walked by."

"So that's why he went quiet."

She smiled at him. "I don't care what he thinks. I like geeks. They are good for helping me with my homework."

"I think the new girl's a geek," he said.

She agreed. "Yes. Ning said she was bookish and all that. Why are some kids so hostile to people who actually like studying? I guess one day they'll find that becoming knowledgeable about stuff is really fun."

"One day," said Jeremiah. "I hope."

Chapter five

WHEN THE BELL RANG for the end of lunch break, Jeri made sure he was the first person through the door of the classroom and was sitting reading a book, already on the second chapter, by the time the teacher entered.

Mrs Suklemon picked up her marker and walked to the whiteboard. But before she could start speaking, there was a knock at the door.

It was Mr Gee, head of mathematics. "Sorry to interrupt your lesson," he said, "but I just wanted to share some good news. An honour for the school, really."

He turned and scanned the children in the class. His gaze settled on Jeremiah, who cringed. Uh-oh.

"For the first time in the history of our school, one of our students has been invited to attend the annual meeting of the NRT, the Nerds Round

Table," he said. "I've just been notified by the organising committee."

"Who is it?" asked Prakash from the front of class.

"Jeremiah Lee," said Mr Gee. "Well done, Jeremiah." He gave Jeremiah a round of applause, but no one joined in.

***

After the end-of-school bell rang, Jeremiah loitered in the school library until most of the other children had gone.

He wasn't feeling very sociable, and decided that he'd rather walk home by himself.

But when the playground was quiet, and he started to head for home, he realised that someone else had the same idea. Crossing the playground, walking backwards by herself, was the new girl, Miranda.

"Hello," he said, catching up with her. "Can I

ask you something?"

"Yes," she said. "You can ask me anything you like. Except you can't ask me why I walk backwards or anything related to that."

"Oh. Okay," he said. He paused.

"Well, do you have anything else to ask me?"

"Um. Sure," he said. "I just wanted to say that I think I saw you yesterday evening. I was, er, wandering around the fields near the farm on the ridge, and I saw a person with light-coloured hair and dark glasses. Was that you?'

"It might have been. I like to go for walks by myself."

"Backwards?" he said.

"Yes," she said.

"Why?" he asked.

"I told you, you're not allowed to ask anything about that."

"Oh yeah. Can I ask you how come you don't bump into things?'

"No."

"Okay, I won't then."

"I gotta go," she said, as they reached the corner of the road.

He noticed that she crossed the roads facing forwards, and looking right and left – clearly she didn't want to put herself in any danger.

When Jeremiah reached home, he found Grandma Nan in her chair doing some knitting. "Did you see that letter on the table?" she said to him. "Looks like you got another invitation."

Oh no, he thought to himself. What was it this time? Another invitation to a geek conference? Or a free membership card to a swots' association? Or an announcement that he had won a competition for nerdiest freak of the year?

He didn't move from his chair.

She looked over at him. "This letter isn't for you, Jeremiah," she said.

He looked up.

"It's for Jeri Telstar," she continued. "It was received at police headquarters, and they sent it to

Officer Bart, who gave it to me."

He raced to the hall table, and picked up the fat envelope. Returning to his chair, he tore it open. The first line of the letter made his eyes widen. *"Dear Superhero,"* it said. *"You are invited to attend a regional conference of superheroes on Volcano Island."*

"Hooray!" said Jeremiah. "Gran, I've been invited to a conference of superheroes. I've made it. I'm legit."

But as his eyes travelled further down the letter to see the details, his face fell. The date was the 14th day of the month – the same day he was supposed to be at the Nerds Round Table. He was double-booked.

***

The following morning, Jeremiah arrived early at school and waited in the playground. He had to find her. She was his only chance.

Luckily, the pale hair made her easy to spot – as did the fact that she walked backwards into school, ignoring the giggles and puzzlement around her.

51

"Miranda, hi, how are you?"

"Terrible," she said. "As usual."

"What's wrong?"

"Nothing," she said. "Except that I really hate this school and I hate this town and I hate my life."

"Oh," he said. "But other than that, everything's fine?"

She glared at him, puzzled at his response. Then she realised that he was joking with her and gave him half a smile.

"Can I talk to you?" he continued.

"You are talking to me."

"About something serious." He walked with her up to the steps towards her classroom. "Miranda, will you do a favour for me?"

"What?"

"I want you to go to the Nerds Round Table in my place."

"Me? No way. You're invited, not me. I've heard about you. You ask the teachers for extra homework."

"How did you know that?"

"Someone told me. Some tall skinny boy. He's a big mouth."

Jeremiah nodded. "Morris Maurice."

"He said that you loved homework books and read them all weekend. He said that you often sat in the library through playtime, because you prefer studying to playing."

"Maybe I do," he said.

Miranda said, "I pretended to be shocked because that's what he seemed to expect my reaction to be."

"But what was your real reaction?"

"I just thought: what a good idea. Sometimes I like to spend playtime in the library."

"You're a swot, too. It's obvious. So will you go in my place?"

"No. No way. I'm not half as bad as you are. They'd find me out."

"No, they wouldn't. All you have to do is go there, sit quietly and listen to the speeches, and then make a short speech yourself."

"I can't make speeches about geeky things."

"You don't have to. I'll write it out for you. All you have to do is read it out loud for me."

She shook her head. "I'm sorry. It's a crazy idea. I would be way out of place."

"But you're already out of place. It seems to me that you're out of place wherever you go. You're just that sort of person."

She blinked. "Yeah, I think that might be true. But why should I do this for you? I only met you yesterday."

"I'm your best friend at this school."

She thought for a moment. "That's only because I'm new and haven't made any friends yet. I still don't see why I should do this for you."

He stopped. He looked in his bag. "I'll tell you why. There's going to be lots of interesting people there, including Casper Chan, son of Dr Erasmus Chan."

"Never heard of him."

"Dr Chan? He's an expert in knee joint injuries," Jeremiah said. "He's an expert in retro-podic exercise and dancing injuries."

She turned and stared at him. "What did you say?"

"Retro-podic exercises and dancing injuries."

"You know?" she said in a small voice.

"Know what?"

"You know who I — I mean, why are you talking about knee joints and stuff?"

He smiled. "The usual. I read it in one of my homework books."

"You're studying medical books at your age?"

He shook his head. "Not medical books. I was reading a history book, actually. Lots of famous boxers, like Muhammad Ali and Gene Tunney, ran backwards for exercise. They call it retro-walking among other things. It helps you fix the leg muscles if you have a knee injury. And it's good for a muscle that has a long name I can't remember. Quad something."

"Quadriceps."

"That's the one. It's good for the quadriceps and the ham-something."

"Hamstrings."

She flexed her feet, pointing her toes straight outwards like a dancer.

"Walking backwards is good for your knees and your thighs and other parts," she said.

"I read that," he replied. "You used to be a dancer and then you hurt yourself, right?"

Now that her secret was no longer secret, she seemed anxious to share information about it.

"In parts of China, it's very common to walk backwards for your health. Thousands of people do it every day," she said. "It's good for your leg muscles, but it is also good for your back and tummy, because it stretches muscles in good ways."

"I read that it also improves peripheral vision."

She turned to him. "You know, Jeremiah Lee, you're a pretty smart guy."

He smiled. "Smart enough to make you look good if you go to the geek meeting for me."

"I'll consider it," she said.

The bell rang. They went their separate ways to their classrooms.

Chapter six

JEREMIAH COULDN'T FIND Volcano Island in his atlas. So he pulled out the invitation letter again and turned to a page that said, "How to get there".

"You will not find Volcano Island in an atlas or on the internet," the letter said. *"That is because it is a private island owned by a superhero, who keeps it well hidden. He keeps it under the surface of the water most of the time, and just brings it up to the surface when he needs it. Simply go to the following coordinates at the designated time."*

Jeremiah flicked to the right page of his atlas. Sure enough, all that could be seen at those coordinates was a patch of sea, about five kilometres away from the coast of Saltwinds.

A quick search of images on the internet showed the same thing. Whoever owned the island made sure that it was out of sight when geographers and photo-taking satellites were passing overhead. Cool.

The details of the conference were interesting. He was intrigued to read that all attendees had to travel by boat. No one was allowed to fly there.

"All attendees will have to report to a clinic that has been set up at the mooring port of Saltwinds' dockside," the letter said. *"There you will undergo a short examination and a DNA reading for purposes of temporary equalisation."*

Jeremiah went back to his computer and looked up "superhero equalisation". The paragraph he read explained it clearly: *"Equalisation is a technique used to temporarily remove powers from gatherings of people with special powers; people such as superheroes and supervillains, for example."*

He wondered why the good guys and the bad guys were lumped together. But then he thought about Musclehead and realised that sometimes there wasn't much of a dividing line between them.

He read on: *"Both superheroes and supervillains tend to be extremely violent people. For this reason, gatherings of 20 or more such people are not allowed unless a vortex is created*

60

at the meeting place where superpowers are temporarily disabled."

This made sense, he realised.

The invitation letter explained that each superhero would be examined at the clinic, and details would be fed into the satellite creating the vortex over Volcano Island. It would cause both natural and artificial superpowers to be disabled for the 12 hours that the conference would run.

***

On Saturday morning, the day of the two conferences, Jeremiah woke early and had breakfast.

After spending a couple of hours reading textbooks, he looked at his watch. It was nearly eight o'clock.

He raced over to the farm where Miranda lived. He rang the doorbell and her father opened the door. "She's upstairs, packing," he said. "Come in."

Jeremiah waited politely downstairs until Miranda appeared.

"I must be crazy doing this for you," she said. "I reckon I am only half the geek you are."

"So why *are* you doing this for me?" he asked.

"Because I know that life is weird, and when someone asks you to help them, sometimes the strangest requests can be the most important. And also, I would like to meet Dr Erasmus Chan one day. He's supposed to be world's greatest expert on injuries among dancers."

"You might meet him today," said Jeremiah. "He'll probably drop off his son at the venue himself. And talking of important things, here's the speech I wrote for you." He got out a small pile of paper and handed it to her.

She scanned the front page. "It looks easy enough. Any hard words in it?"

"No, it's all pretty simple," he said.

"You sure they won't be expecting a boy?"

"I already called the organiser and said that our

school was sending you in my place. They're fine with that."

"I'm still nervous. What if it all goes wrong? You promise you'll come and rescue me?"

"I promise," he said.

He took a sheet of paper and wrote out a number. "Call this number and you'll get straight through to me. You have any problems at all, and I will drop what I am doing and come straight over to save you."

"What are you doing anyway? Why can't you go to this?"

"It's a secret and it's important."

"How important?"

"Important to me, but not so important that I wouldn't drop it in a moment and come running if you need me."

"Thanks, Jeremiah," she said.

He said goodbye to her and then – just to see how it felt – walked backwards all the way home.

One hour later, Jeri Telstar was soaring through the sky. He was so excited he could hardly contain himself.

This was the moment. This was when he was officially going to be recognised as a superhero. He had been invited to a gathering of the region's most important costumed crime fighters. All the main players in the business would be there. He would meet the stars, he would get some autographs. He would be recognised as "one of them". He would be photographed by the press in the presence of people who had been superheroes for years, or decades, even.

A minute later, he arrived at the dockside of Saltwinds.

His visit to the clinic took barely ten minutes. After he had explained to the doctors and nurses that his powers were artificial rather than natural, the equalisation process was easy. His boots and equipment worked on nanotechnology, created by Grandma Nan and her two helpers, Nan Two and

Nan Three. Nanotechology was the science of tiny motors – motors that worked by electricity or by chemicals acting on each other or by molecules responding to other molecules. His boots had tiny rocket motors in them that kept him flying through the air. The doctors explained that his superpowers would be disabled for at least 12 hours.

He emerged from the clinic and found himself standing at the boarding gate next to a female superhero he didn't recognise.

"Hi," she said. "I'm Hypo Allergenic Woman. You can call me Hype."

"My name's Jeri Telstar."

A young man with a rubber head approached them. "I'm the Mistake Eradicator," he said, shaking both their hands.

A man wider than he was tall came through the door – removing the door frame in the process. "Oops! Greetings, fellow heroes," he said. "I am the Impervious Brute."

"Didn't I used to be married to you?" asked Hypo Allergenic Woman.

"Maybe," said the Impervious Brute. "Or one of my brothers. I come from a big family. When we all get together, we're known as the Brute Force."

"Nice," said the Mistake Eradicator.

A woman with a large mouth on her chest logo approached and kneeled down to look at Jeri. "Hi, sweetheart," she said. "I'm the Underrated Venomous Banshee. I can knock people over by screaming. Who are you, and what's your power?"

"My name's Jeri Telstar. I've got a suit powered by nano-motors. I can fly and stuff. Well, not at the moment, of course."

"Is that your only power? Nano-motors?"

"Actually, I solve most of my cases using stuff I learn in textbooks. Some people call me the Homework Hero," he said.

"I like that," she replied. "It's different."

***

Only six of them were on the boat to Volcano Island.

The Mistake Eradicator was puzzled as to why there were so few.

"Maybe the others have their own boats," Jeri suggested.

Hypo Allergenic Woman nodded. "Too right. Most superheroes, especially male ones, have massive egos. I bet most of them have fancy yachts."

Minutes later, the boat started rocking in the waves, as a huge triple-deck motorised yacht swept past them.

The Banshee studied the logo on the boat. "That's the Deep Fried Titan," she said. "He's even more of an egomaniac than Musclehead. Musclehead's got a huge boat."

The other adult heroes nodded. Jeri felt his heartbeat speed up. He wasn't looking forward to seeing Musclehead again.

When they arrived at Volcano Island, they

noticed that there were several dozen vessels of various sizes moored to the dockside, including motor cruisers, yachts and jet-skis.

The first thing the six of them saw when they got off their boat was Musclehead having an argument with the staff on the island.

"I'm sorry," a staff member was telling him. "You cannot bring your musical group here. If you want your theme music played before you speak, you can give a disk to the organiser."

The superhero growled and spat on the sand, before walking with other heroes towards the main hall in the centre of the beach.

Jeri's worries were soon forgotten as he watched, wide-eyed with amazement, as several of the most famous heroes in the region appeared on the shore.

Walking up the beach to his right was the Unpredictable Bananaman, jogging along in his yellow costume. To his left he saw the Inflatable Gymnast, followed by her equally famous husband, Hop, Skip and Jump Man.

Jeri wondered if it would be uncool to collect autographs while he was at the meeting.

He started looking in his backpack for an exercise book and a pen, but they almost immediately arrived at the main hall and were ushered into a large auditorium, where rows of seats faced a grand stage.

"Who organised this meeting anyway?" Hypo Allergenic Woman asked out loud, to no one in particular.

"I guess it must be the World Association of Heroes," said Deep Fried Titan.

An old woman in a leotard interrupted. "Actually, I'm the committee leader of the Association this year, and it wasn't us."

"Perhaps it was the Superheroes' Union," said the Impervious Brute.

A young man in a leotard behind them called out: "Nope. I'm their representative, and it wasn't us."

"Maybe it's some sort of new society of supers," said Hypo Allergenic Woman. "Oh well, I guess we'll find out soon enough."

After a few minutes, the lights went down in the stalls, and glowed bright on the stage. The curtains opened and a figure stepped out. It seemed to be a large man encased in a bright yellow costume that covered him from head to toe.

"Welcome, ladies and gentlemen, to the first meeting of the Regional Council of Superheroes," he said in a deep voice. "I am the Mystifying Mega Mango, and I am your host today. I am thrilled that you all managed to make it here."

There was a polite round of applause.

"I most sincerely thank you for coming," he said. "We've got a great turnout. The majority of the region's finest superheroes are right here in this room. It's a great honour to have you all here. Before we start, I want to ask you to turn off your communication devices."

There was a chorus of grumbles at this.

"I know, I know," said Mystifying Mega Mango. "We're all the same. None of us are used to being out of touch with our communities. But I feel it is important for all of us that we take a break from saving people and have a bit of time to ourselves. You owe it to yourselves. So please, turn all your phones and similar devices off."

There was a chorus of beeps as machines were reluctantly powered down.

Jeri turned to his wrist communicator and his finger hovered over the "off" button.

But how could he turn it off? He had *promised* Miranda that he would keep it on. He had pledged to her that he would be available for her if she needed him at a moment's notice.

He moved his finger away from it. Perhaps no one would notice.

"Now come on, don't hesitate," the man on stage said. "I know some of you will be tempted to leave them on. But be strong. Turn them off. Your home communities need to learn to stand on their own feet for short periods."

Jeri's finger went back to the communicator and hovered over the "off" button again.

There were more audible beeps of devices being powered down.

"Good," said the man in orange. "Now I want everyone to–"

"Who are you?" the Impervious Brute shouted out. "How come we've never heard of you before?"

"Good question," said the mango-coloured man. "Well, let me just say this. Everything will become perfectly clear to all of us at 10am. But first let me say that–"

"Hey! Can I say something?" Musclehead stood up in his seat and was shouting at the top of his voice. "I got something really important to say."

The Mango Man said: "Thank you, Mr Musclehead. We are honoured to have such a famous hero with us. There will be plenty of time for discussions later, I assure you. We have a packed schedule."

Musclehead waved his hand in a gesture of irritation. "Never mind the schedule. This is important. Last week I was totally humiliated – humiliated in front of live TV cameras, and that means in front of millions of people. And if someone as great as me can be made a fool of, it could happen to any of you, for sure."

"Let's discuss it later," the masked man on stage said.

"What happened?" the Deep Fried Titan asked Musclehead.

"Yeah, tell us about it," said the Inflatable Gymnast.

Musclehead's voice became high-pitched and he sounded emotional and vulnerable as he recalled what was clearly a shocking memory. "Well, I was doing my job, right in the middle of an important rescue, saving a small no-good town that didn't deserve to be saved, when this kid shows up. Some sort of little hero kid."

"Who?" someone shouted.

"Don't remember his name. Joe Television or something. Anyway, some little kid with a mask on. He claims to be a superhero but he doesn't seem to even have any powers. And then – and then – he totally humiliated me. He said that you solved problems using things you learn instead of just brute strength."

"That's outrageous," said the Impervious Brute.

"This kid has no respect for traditional superhero values, like smashing through walls, hitting people and throwing heavy objects."

"Shocking," said the Mistake Eradicator.

"And then he pushed me aside and solved the problem without using any sort of superpower at all – and all in front of the TV cameras."

Musclehead sniffed, his voice cracking at the memory of it. A sympathetic silence descended on the audience.

Jeri was sneaking backwards out of the room at this point. Walking backwards was actually a rather useful technique when you want to exit without being noticed, he realised. He had just reached the back of the auditorium when his wrist phone came to life.

Beep beep beep beep.

The Mango Man on the stage looked annoyed. "All communication devices are supposed to be off at this time," he thundered.

Everyone's eyes turned to the back of the auditorium.

In the silence, a tiny voice could be heard coming out of Jeri's wrist monitor: "Call for Jeri Telstar. Call for Jeri Telstar."

Musclehead turned round and stared. "That's him," he said. "That's the kid."

"Oops," said Jeri.

Chapter seven

THE MEETING ERUPTED INTO SHOUTS.

"Stop him!"

"Who?"

"Him. There."

"Where'd he go?"

"After him!"

Jeri raced down the hall towards the exit doors, reckoning that he would be safer out on the beach than stuck in an auditorium with Musclehead and 50 of his furious friends.

From his wrist, he heard Miranda's voice. "Jeremiah? Are you there? Jeremiah?"

"Yeah, I'm, er, right here," he said, running along the corridor.

"I need your help."

"Can I get back to you?'

"It's really urgent."

"I'll just put you on hold for a second, then, and

get back to you very soon."

Although he knew that some of the superheroes, if they heard his side of the story, might be sympathetic to him, he realised that he wouldn't get a chance to give any sort of explanation in this angry mob situation.

Jeri reached the exit doors and ran onto the beach.

Hot on his heels, he could hear Musclehead and his friends panting behind him.

The boy ran up to the edge of the docking pier, but then there was nowhere else to go. He stopped and turned.

Musclehead strode up to him, his weight causing the pier to shake with every footstep. Right behind were his equally frightening looking buddies, including Deep Fried Titan and the Impervious Brute.

"Now I'm gonna show you why a real superhero needs muscles," Musclehead roared. "You followed me here to humiliate me again, right?"

"No, sir, not at all, sir," said Jeri.

"Do you deny that you totally humiliated me last week?"

"Er, no, I guess technically speaking I did totally humiliate you. But I didn't mean to."

"There! He admits it! His mission is to pour scorn on traditional superheroes and our traditional strength-based methods."

He took a step closer.

Jeri pressed the button that turned his superpowers on just to see if anything would happen. Nothing. The entire suit had been disabled at the equalisation clinic.

He could hear Mystifying Mega Mango shouting from the back. "Excuse me, ladies and gentleman. I'd like you all to come back into the auditorium. We have a very special announcement to make at exactly 10 o'clock and it's almost that time now."

Ignoring him, Musclehead took a step towards Jeri.

Hypo Allergenic Woman leaped in between the

pair of them.

"Back off, Musclehead," she said. "You can't beat him up. He's just a kid. Besides, it's hard to humiliate you more than you humiliate yourself. I mean look at your name: Musclehead. I mean really!"

"Get out of the way, Hype. I ain't gonna beat him up. I'm gonna throw him off this island. He don't respect superhero traditions. He don't deserve to be here."

Jeri's wrist phone rang again. Miranda must have rung off and then called again. He heard her voice, now sharp and angry. "Jeremiah? Are you there? You said you would come if I needed you. I need you now! Right now! Please."

"Hi, Miranda, I'll talk to you very soon," he said. "Just wait ten seconds. Please. This is a life or death situation."

"So is this," she said. "I've lost the papers you gave me and the meeting is about to start."

He put her on hold again and scanned the faces

around him.

There were now dozens of superheroes standing around watching the confrontation. His reputation was at stake.

Should he stay and argue the case with Musclehead? If this was a movie, he would make a big speech about the importance of avoiding violence if at all possible, and stirring music would be played in the background, and everyone watching would start to realise that he was not a bad guy, but a hero.

But life was not a movie. He couldn't think of anything to say. All he could think of was that he had promised to respond immediately to a cry of help from Miranda, and he had to find a way of doing it – and stay alive, if possible.

Hypo Allergenic Woman put her hands on her hips and shouted in Musclehead's face. "Leave the kid alone. You're just a big bully, and you know what I think? Maybe the kid is right. Maybe we supers are too quick to choose hitting people as an answer to every problem."

"Er, excuse me," Jeri said. "I have to go now."

He walked backwards towards the edge of the pier. Walking backwards was surprisingly easy. You just had to clearly picture in your head what you had seen behind you.

Musclehead sneered at him. "That's right. Run away. That's all your type can do when you face a *real* problem. Run. Ha ha ha."

Jeri turned and jumped off the pier onto a jet ski.

He pressed the ignition button and was soon soaring at top speed towards the Saltwinds' coastline.

***

Jeri was less than a minute away from the island when he heard a huge explosion behind him.

There was a second explosion, then a third.

He spun his head round to see what had happened.

All the high-powered superhero boats around the island were exploding, one by one.

Bang! There went Deep Fried Titan's triple-deck superyacht.

Pow! There went Musclehead's *Flying Fist*.

Whump! There went the Inflatable Gymnast's speedcruiser.

Jeri glanced at his watch and noticed that it was exactly 10am. The mooring posts of the island had been lined with explosives. The mango guy had been saying that there would be a surprise at 10am. This must be it.

Jeri stopped the jet ski and spun it round so he could see what was happening.

"What's going on?" shouted the Impervious Brute.

"That boat cost a fortune," yelled Deep Fried Titan. "I put all my Hollywood payments into that boat."

Some of the heroes just wept, as their burning luxury yachts sank.

Hypo Allergenic Woman seemed to have realised that something very wrong was happening. "This is a trap. We need to find some way to turn off the equalisation vortex," she shouted. "We need to get our powers back!"

***

But it was too late. The man in the mango-coloured clothes had disappeared. Seconds later he reappeared – on a balcony below the roof of the meeting building.

In one sweeping move, he threw off his mango costume. Underneath, he wore a black martial arts outfit. The only bits of skin you could see were his hands and his eyes – and both were a horrible, glistening greenish colour.

There was a gasp from all the superheroes below him.

"Yes, it's me," he said. "The Unpalatable Slime." The Mistake Eradicator spoke everyone's thoughts

out loud: "This whole thing has been a trick to get us marooned with no powers!"

"Correct," said the Unpalatable Slime. "There is no new Regional Superheroes' Association. I drew you all here and persuaded you to subject yourselves to the equalisation process to rob you of your powers."

He raised both fists in the air. "At last! At last!" He exulted. "All power is mine! Mine!" He gave an evil laugh. "Mwah ha ha ha ha."

"Isn't he overdoing it a bit?" the Underrated Venomous Banshee said.

Hypo Allergenic Woman nodded. "Yeah. But he's a supervillain. They're all hams."

The Mistake Eradicator said, "And you must admit, he's right. He's tricked us all into giving up our powers and now we're trapped on this island with no method of getting away."

"It's pretty clever," said the Impervious Brute.

There was a general murmur of approval. No one was happy at being trapped, but they were willing to give due credit to the villain's planning and organisational abilities.

The Unpalatable Slime said, "You may be wondering what's going to happen next? Well, I shall tell you. My supervillain henchmen are waiting on the shore, at the nearby town of Saltwinds. I will leave you rotting on this island and join them, and then we will go robbing and plundering to our hearts' content. Without you to protect them, the citizens of the world will not be able to protect themselves. I can help myself to the best of everything. I can completely empty shops of goods. I can fill my pockets with money from the banks. I can do anything I want. And I can blacken your names, as the populace will cry for you to come and rescue them, and their calls will go unheeded. Mwah ha ha ha!"

He disappeared from the balcony.

"Where do you think he's gone?" Hop, Skip and Jump Man asked.

"He's destroyed all our boats," said Hypo Allergenic Woman. "There must have been bombs planted all the way along the mooring pier. But he's probably got his own boat hidden away safe somewhere, probably in a private bay on the other side of the island. Like in the James Bond movies."

Just then, Deep Fried Titan appeared from around the edge of the building. "Correction," he said. "The Unpalatable Slime *had* his own boat hidden away in a private bay on the other side of the island. I just went and kicked in the boat's hull. There's no way he can sail away in it. He's trapped here with us."

The Underrated Venomous Banshee sat down on the sand. "Well, if none of us can leave the island, we may as well relax."

The Impervious Brute gazed across the water in the direction of the land. "How far is it to the shore?" he asked. "Can we swim there?"

"It's too far," said Deep Fried Titan.

"Will someone come and save us?"

"Who? Every superhero in the region is here."

"Not every superhero," said Hypo Allergenic Woman.

Chapter eight

BOBBING UP AND DOWN on his jet ski on the open ocean, Jeri released that it was up to him to save the superheroes of the region – even though they had been so mean to him.

But there was one thing he had to do first: he must fulfill his promise to Miranda.

He turned the jet ski around again and headed southwest, to the annual round table conference of swots.

He clicked on his wrist phone. "Miranda? Are you there?"

"Hi, Jeri. Are you on your way? There's only ten minutes to go before I am due to speak. Have you got a spare copy of your paper?"

"No need for that. I'm going to propose that the round table members do something different from what's on the schedule. There's a bit of an emergency happening out here, and we need you all to help."

"I'm not sure if this gang will help," Miranda said. "They're kind of a weird bunch. When will you be here?"

"In five minutes. Over and out."

***

Exactly four and a half minutes later, Jeri skidded the jet ski to a halt on the beach at Saltwinds and raced up the sandy slopes to the library in the town hall.

Running up the stairs, he burst into the room.

Twelve faces, all rather intense and bookish, turned to stare at him.

"Excuse me," he said. "You don't know me, but – "

"I know you," said a small boy with owlish glasses. "You're Jeri Telstar. A junior superhero based in the town of Utter Backwater. Regional super-persons is one of my special subjects in inter-school quiz rounds."

"Interesting. You must tell me more about it – later. At the moment, there's a crisis going on and your help is needed."

A girl put up her hand. "My specialist subject includes disasters and crises. I know all about them. Is there any particular historical crisis that you want more information on?"

"Not just now," said Jeri. "This crisis is just

about to happen. It's a new one."

She looked disappointed. "I don't think I can help you then."

"No, wait. You can help. You can all help. We need you to help."

A large boy wearing a bow tie stood up. "I'm Billy Bok, the chairperson of this meeting, so please address your comments through the chair. What is the crisis and why do you need us? May I remind you that this is a meeting of the NRT—"

"I know, I know."

"You are not entitled to—"

The girl who liked disasters said: "At least we should let him tell us what the crisis is. Maybe we'll want to be involved."

"Only if it is intellectually stimulating, which I doubt it will be," sneered the chairperson, looking at Jeri.

The story burst out of Jeri: "One of the world's most dangerous supervillains, a man called the Unpalatable Slime, has captured almost every superhero in the region and placed them on an island about four kilometres northeast of here. He plans to rob all the banks in the region while they are trapped on the island."

"Surely they can escape," said Billy Bok. "They are superheroes, after all, aren't they?"

"They all voluntarily went through an equaliser process," said Jeri.

"I know what that is," said the small, owlish boy. "It's a device that robs heroes of their powers."

"What do you want us to do?" a tall girl standing at the back asked. "Is the Mistake Eradicator there? He's my favourite superhero. He's so cute."

"He's there," said Jeri. "I'm sure he'll give you his autograph."

A boy next to her added: "What about Deep Fried Titan?"

"He's there too."

"Let's go."

As they raced to the doors, the owlish boy asked the question that was probably on everyone's minds: "We're just kids, and worse still, we're swots. How can we fight a real supervillain? I can't even fight girls my own age."

"I don't expect you to use your fists. We're going to work in a different way. We're going to use a secret weapon," said Jeri.

"What's that?" asked the chairperson, still skeptical.

"Our brains," said Jeri. "If any of you are carrying textbooks, bring them along."

His wrist monitor started flashing. The machine announced a call: "Call for Jeri Telstar! Call for Jeri Telstar!"

He clicked it on. "Yes?"

"Hello, young Telstar."

It was the Unpalatable Slime.

"How did you get this number?" Jeri asked.

"Remember, I am the organiser of the superheroes' conference. I have all the forms you filled in right in front of me."

"Bother."

"Now, young Telstar, you are the only superhero to escape from my trap. But I order you to come back right now."

"Of course I won't. Who are you kidding? It's up to me to save everyone."

"You? Ha! You and what army?"

"Me and this army," said Jeri. He stepped aside so that the Slime could see the group of youngsters behind him through the tiny screen.

"They're just a group of kids," the evil supervillain said.

"Correction," said the tall girl. "We are the Nerds Round Table. And we are strange and dangerous weirdos. Everybody says so."

The Unpalatable Slime laughed. "You will come back, Master Telstar. And you can bring your friends with you. I need a few more slaves. Now my turn to show you something. Look at this."

The Slime stepped back and allowed the

camera to focus on something behind him.

Jeri stared. It was Hypo Allergenic Woman. She had been tied up.

"I believe this woman is your friend. Unless you come back to the island and give yourself up right now, she will be stuffed into a cannon and blown into the open sea."

"You wouldn't dare."

"I would. I am a bad guy remember. Mwah ha ha ha ha! You have 20 minutes."

***

Nineteen minutes later, a small speed boat was zooming along the water's edge close to Volcano Island.

As the beach came into view, Miranda said, "You didn't tell me you were a superhero."

"It's a secret. You didn't tell me you were a dancer."

"You worked it out by yourself."

"And you've just worked out who I am."

"I'll keep your secret and you keep mine. Should we keep our heads down too?"

"No need," said Jeri. "We're going to give ourselves up."

"Why? I thought we were going to fight the bad guy and rescue the superheroes?"

"We are. But we're not going to fight with our fists."

"Good," she said. "Because I don't think any of us have any talent in that direction."

Coming up behind them, the nerds' chairperson Billy Bok approached, having heard the last part of the conversation. He folded his arms and looked cross. "I don't think it's smart to give ourselves up. Surely we should try to do something clever?"

"Maybe later," said Jeri. "Just now we can't risk it. They have Hypo Allergenic Woman. We need to make sure she isn't hurt. We have to give ourselves up. Then we'll see what we can do."

"That sounds defeatist to me."

"No. Think about it," said Miranda. "If we join them on the island, who are the strongest people on there?"

"They are," said the boy.

"No, we are."

"How do you work that out?"

"Well, superheroes and supervillains normally have amazing powers. They are not used to operating without them. They are completely at a loss."

The boy said: "But we've never had superpowers to begin with."

"Exactly. We've never had them so we don't miss them. But we've got our brains and our school textbooks – those are the things that have made us special. So we are still ahead of normal people. And way ahead of confused superheroes who have been stripped of their powers. Get it?"

"I get it," Billy said.

Jeri looked at Miranda with new admiration. "You're a smart thinker," he said.

Chapter nine

TEN MINUTES LATER, the swots were on the island, having given themselves up.

The Unpalatable Slime and his henchman had given them jobs. "Since you are small and weak and not dangerous at all, you will become my slaves," he said. "I want six of you to fix my boat.

Some idiot has kicked holes in it. And I want the other six to help me make sure the superheroes are properly secured so that they cannot escape. Do you understand? I'll give each group three hours to finish their project."

"Okay," said Jeri. "I'll lead the boat building group. Miranda, you work with the other group."

***

The boat was badly damaged. It lay on its side, halfway out of the water.

But fortunately there were plenty of trees in the forested part of the island. The team didn't even have to cut them down. The forest was so wild and neglected that there were plenty of fallen trees that had not been cleared.

The young people dragged some of them over to the broken boat. The building had plenty of tools in its workshop, including machine saws, so it was easy to slice the logs into planks that they could use.

One of the girls was the daughter of a carpenter and oversaw the cutting operation. Soon the broken hull of the boat was replaced by fresh new planks.

The operation took several hours, but the team did a good job.

Once the operation was finished, the Unpalatable Slime came to inspect the work.

"Now I want to make sure that you have not tricked me," he said. "Is this boat seaworthy? Have you drilled holes into it? Have you stuck in some sort of remote control plug?"

"No, sir," said the girl who had been in charge of the operation. "We have replaced not only the broken planks, but many of the planks that were looking a bit worn and torn – in fact, you could say that it was more or less a new boat."

The supervillain got a jug and poured liquid over the hull to make sure it was watertight. After ten minutes of tests, the villain decided that the children had down the job properly.

"You've done your work well," he said. "No leaks. Very quick and efficient. Would any of you like to come over to the dark side and be a villain? There is always room for young, evil talent."

"No, thank you, sir, but thanks for offering," Jeri said.

The supervillain slunk away. "Time to go and visit my other prisoners."

***

Miranda and her team had done their jobs
well too. They had used wheelbarrows to pick up
boulders from the side of the volcano and bring
them back to the beach. They had then chained
each superhero to a large rock.

The Unpalatable Slime was as suspicious as ever.

"Are the chains really tight?" he said. "I shall
check each one. And then I shall keep all the keys
myself."

He checked them one by one. Each was securely
locked.

"Now, where are the keys?"

"Here, they are, sir," said Miranda. She handed him a large ring of keys.

"I want both sets."

She handed over a second set.

Satisfied, he gave her the same compliment he had given the others. "Excellent work, young lady. If you or any of your teammates ever wants a job in villainy, I'm sure I will be able to find an opening."

The supervillain, jingling the keys, waved to his henchmen and walked back in the direction of the place where his re-built boat was standing.

Musclehead was furious. "Release me from this rock this instant," he shouted at the children.

"We don't have the keys," Miranda said.

"How dare you chain me up like this!" shouted Deep Fried Titan.

"Leave them alone," said the Hop, Skip and Jump Man. "They're only kids. We can't expect them to fight one of the most dangerous supervillains on earth by themselves."

Musclehead turned to the other heroes and said: "Hah! All this proves that I was right. I told you that Jeri guy was bad news. Hitting people – that's the way to get results."

The Underrated Venomous Banshee turned to him. "Well it hasn't worked for you, has it? You're all chained up here like the rest of us, and you hit people more than anyone."

"Yeah, she's right," said the Mistake Eradicator. "We've all done our work mainly by hitting people, and look where it's got us: stuck here in chains while that villain goes off to plunder our hometowns to his heart's delight."

Musclehead said: "Well, sometimes I win and sometimes I lose. But at least hitting people makes me feel good. But brains? Where do they get you? These kids have got brains but they're worse off than we are. They're actually helping the villain."

"Shh," said the Impervious Brute. "Here comes the Unpalatable Slime."

The supervillain marched to the shore. "My boat is ready. My men are ready. The world is out there, ready for me to plunder. There is nothing to stop me. Particularly not you lot – stuck to rocks as you are. Goodbye and good riddance."

He turned to the children. "Thanks for all your help. I have left my email address with young Telstar. If any of you want further employment as junior villains, drop me a note."

Musclehead shouted out: "Don't take the keys. You can't leave us trapped here forever."

"I'm not planning on taking the keys with me," said the supervillain. "I know exactly where I am going to put them."

He took the two rings of keys and dropped them into the cannon. He pulled the firing pin and there was a loud boom. The keys flew into the air and soared out over the sea. They landed so far away that no one could hear the splash.

"The keys are gone forever. I may return one day with a spare set and set you free. Or I may never return. In which case, the children can feed you with bananas from the trees. That's all you monkeys deserve."

He turned and signalled to his henchmen to start the boat's engines. After a few seconds, there was a steady chugging noise, and the boat started to churn up the water.

Minutes later, it sailed off towards the coast with its cargo of excited robbers.

***

"What are we going to do?" said Deep Fried Titan.

"Let me try and use my muscles to break these chains," said Musclehead.

"Excuse me, sir," Jeri said.

"Don't bother me kid. I'm busy."

"I know. Excuse me, but–"

"I said don't bother me. Can't you see that what I am doing is the only chance we have of saving our communities? After you caused all the trouble I thought you would be smart enough to stay out of our way."

"That's not fair," said Hypo Allergenic Woman. "The kids didn't cause the trouble. It was our stupidity that caused us to get into this mess. Fancy us all agreeing to go through that equalisation process."

"Er, excuse me," Jeri said, louder this time. He climbed on to the boulder that was chained to the Inflatable Gymnast. "I have an announcement to make."

"Shut up," said Musclehead.

"No, let's listen to what he has to say," said the Mistake Eradicator.

"I have some important information. We used wood from the local forests to fix the boat of the Unpalatable Slime."

"We know that."

"We chose the wood very carefully. As you know, wood is a substance made of plant cellulose that floats on water."

"Shut up. This is not the time to show off your blasted biology homework."

"But what some people do not know is that not all wood floats," Jeri continued. "In fact, there is a type of wood that is unusually heavy and sinks in water."

The superheroes stopped struggling and stared at the young boy.

"It only grows in old forests, and we were delighted to find some samples of it among the fallen trees here. We used this textbook (he held up his biology textbook) to identify it.

It is a type of black ironwood with a scientific name of *Olea laurifolia*."

"What are you saying?"

"We replaced most of the planking in the Unpalatable Slime's boat with planks made from this type of wood."

Musclehead said: "Are you saying that the Slime's boat will sink?"

"In fact, I expect it has already started sinking."

"Look!" said the Unpredictable Bananaman.

Everyone stood up. The boat was still heading towards the land – but it was floating low in the water. The sea was already almost up to the deck railings.

"I calculate that in about three minutes, the sailors will notice and panic," said Jeri. "They will then spend some minutes looking for a leak."

"But they won't find one," added Miranda.

"Because there isn't one. Most people cannot imagine a wooden boat not being able to float, so they will look in vain for a leak. In fact, there is nothing they can do that will stop the boat sinking."

Bananaman laughed: "One of the sailors is staring over the side. He's talking to his friends. I think they are already starting to panic."

"Is there a lifeboat there?" Hypo Allergenic Woman asked.

"Yes, there's a lifeboat," said Jeri. "So the Slime and his henchmen will end up floating in it."

Miranda added: "But the lifeboat has no oars – we removed them – so that they will have to stay there bobbing in the water until they are rescued."

"Who by?" said Musclehead.

"By us," said Jeri.

"May I just remind you that you have chained us to these rocks, and the keys have been thrown into the ocean?"

Miranda stood up.

"For the second part of the plan, we used this textbook."

She held up a book with a picture of a mountain on it. "This is a textbook that forms part of the geography syllabus. It is called *Beginner's Geology*."

"It's about rocks," Musclehead deduced. "Well, you should know all about rocks, since you chained us to them."

"Rocks, as you know, are extremely heavy items that immediately sink to the bottom when dropped into the sea," Miranda continued.

"Even I knew that," said Musclehead.

"Except for one type."

There was a moment of silence.

She continued: "We learned that there is one type of rock that has a density less than water. It floats. It is called pumice. Scientists refer to it as an extrusive vesicular igneous rock. It is generally found near volcanos."

Hypo Allergenic Woman stood up. "Is this it?" she asked.

Jeri said: "If you try pulling at your rock, you'll find it is much lighter than you expect."

"She's right," said the Unpredictable Bananaman. "I can actually lift this boulder up."

"You can use it as a float," said Miranda.

Musclehead was already running to the beach holding his rock. "We got floats," he said. "We can swim off this island."

"We can swim to Saltwinds' beach," said the Impervious Brute.

"We can swim to the Unpalatable Slime's

lifeboat and tell him what we think of him," said the Unpredictable Bananaman.

"We can swim out of the range of the equaliser and get our powers back – and use our super-strength to break these chains!" said Deep Fried Titan. "We're free!"

They raced down the beach after Musclehead.

Chapter ten

SCHOOL ASSEMBLY ON Monday morning was
as dull as ever.

Then the headmaster, Mr Ning, said: "Now I
believe we have a student who went to the Nerds
Round Table at Saltwinds' beach this weekend.
Who was it?"

"Jeremiah Lee," some of the children shouted out.

Mr Gee, the maths teacher, raised his hand.
"Actually, I believe Miranda Tuck went in his
place."

Jeremiah said, "We both went in the end."

There was a lot of giggling in the room, and
Jeremiah could hear someone starting a chant of
"Losers, losers" in the back of the hall.

"Hush, children," said Mr Ning. "Now you may
think that young people who actually find some
enjoyment in studying, even on their weekends,
are what you might call losers."

"Yes!" shouted a group of kids at the back. "Losers!" several of them added.

"But I think you might be surprised at what transpired," the headmaster continued. "I noticed this news item on the television last night, and I used the video machine to record it." He looked at the technician at the back of the room. "Can you play the tape, please, John?"

The lights went down, and up on the screen at the front of the hall came a news clip.

A news anchor was speaking. "An evil supervillain named The Unpalatable Slime captured many of the region's most respected superheroes this weekend, including Musclehead and the Unpredictable Bananaman," the news reporter said.

"But they escaped from their bonds, and after a pitched battle in the waters off the coast of Saltwinds, managed to subdue the bad guy and take him and his henchmen into custody. Here's a report from the scene."

Up on the screen came an image of Hypo Allergenic Woman wrenching her chains apart. "This was the toughest battle of our lives," she told the reporter. "Our super-strength was of no use at all. We triumphed only because there were some people among us who had done their homework. I'd like to take the opportunity to thank the members of the Nerds Round Table, who were on the spot and provided the crucial help that made all the difference. Without their knowledge, we would have lost the battle."

There was stunned silence in the hall.

"So, well done, young swots," Mr Ning said, starting a round of applause.

***

In the playground, Morris Maurice approached Jeremiah, who was chatting with Miranda. "Hi, Jeremiah. I'm thinking of starting a new club. Want to join?"

"What happened to your Secret Club?" Jeremiah asked.

"Oh, it fell to bits. By the end of Friday, almost everybody in school was a member, so none of the secrets were secret any more. So we abandoned it."

"Too bad."

"But I got a new club. Wanna join?"

"I don't think so."

"You'd like it. It's called the Help-A-Hero club. We meet after school in the library and go through the books and do fun research and stuff to help local heroes do their job."

Jeri looked puzzled. "But that's what I already do. Me and Merry started that club ages ago. And Miranda's joined us too."

"Can I join?"

"Listen, Morris," said Jeremiah. "You don't need to join anything to get fun out of studying things. Any kid who realises that knowledge is not uncool – but the coolest thing on the planet – is automatically a member.

"Cool! So I'm a member?"

"You might be, if you're serious about it."

Morris nodded, and then raced off to tell Loretta that he was in a new club.

"Now can I ask a question about your walking backwards?" Jeremiah said.

"Sure."

"Why do you wear tinted glasses?"

"They have little mirrors in the sides that help me not bump into things when I walk backwards. I've got a spare pair you can borrow."

The two of them walked backwards all the way to Miranda's house.

StarFacts

IN THIS STORY, JERI helped the superheroes learn that problems should be solved with your brains, not your fists.

Here are some true facts from this book that can help you be a Homework Hero too.

✦ **ARCHIMEDES** was a man who worked out the easiest way to measure the mass of something. Put it into water and see how much the water level goes up.

✦ **YOU CAN TRY THE SALT EXPERIMENT AT HOME.** Put some salt in the bottom of a bottle, and then pour water on top, until it is nearly full. Mark the level on the bottle, and then shake the bottle to dissolve the salt. What happens to the level of the water? The level will go down! This is because the salt occupies space in the bottle and the liquid level will drop as the salt is dissolved in the water.

✦ When Jeri uses the thread to take water away from the tank, he is using a very special property of water called **SURFACE TENSION**. This is the reason that water collects in drops, but it is also why water can travel up a plant stem, or get to your cells through the smallest blood vessels.

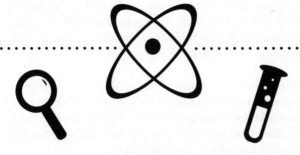

+ **WALKING BACKWARDS** is an exercise
  that many sports people do, and it's good
  for dancers who have injured their legs, like
  Miranda in the story. In China, many people
  make walking backwards part of their normal
  exercise routine.

+ **WOOD FLOATS.** But there are a small
  number of types of wood that are so heavy
  that they sink. This includes ironwood, which
  Jeri uses in the story. In fact, the *Guinness
  World Records* lists this tree as the world's
  heaviest wood!

+ **ROCKS SINK.** But the density of pumice,
  a rock that comes from volcanoes, is so low
  that it actually floats on water!

Want to save the world? Are you good at making up stories? If you'd like to suggest an exciting mission for Jeri Telstar, write to us with your ideas. The best ones will win a prize from *PPP*, the company that publishes the *Jeri Telstar* books, and may even appear in a future story. . . You can contact us at *inquiries@ppp.com.hk*.

The author, *Nury Vittachi*, also known as *Mr Jam*, was born on earth and still spends most of his time there. He's written lots of books and also has columns in many newspapers and magazines around the world. When he's on this planet he may visit your school. Ask your teacher to invite him through his website, *www.mrjam.org*.

• •

'A bestselling English-language author based in Hong Kong, Vittachi stands to become a lot better known in the US . . . Vittachi's unique world view infuses his writing with vitality and gives his characters a charming believability'
Publishers Weekly

'The brilliant Vittachi's nerdy hero is back to prove once again that the most powerful forces in the universe are not flying fists but secrets found in books'
Young Booklover

'Your kids will warm to Jeremiah Lee (aka Jeri Telstar)'
Young Parents

'To many, he is Asia's funniest, most pungent columnist and author'
The Herald-Sun, Melbourne

'The delightful, entertaining, and always funny Nury Vittachi, a literary force in Asia'
City Weekend, Shanghai

'The beat reporter of the offbeat'
CNN